The story of *The Little Red Hen* has
been passed down for generations.
There are many versions of the story.
The following tale is a retelling of the
original version. While the story has
been cut for length and level, the basic
elements of the classic tale remain.

The little red hen had a full house.

LITTLE
RED
HEN

4

The Little Red Hen

Retold by Christianne Jones

Illustrated by Natalie Magnuson

www.raintreepublishers.co.uk
Visit our website to find out
more information about
Raintree books.

To order:
Phone 0845 6044371
Fax +44 (0) 1865 312263
Email myorders@raintreepublishers.co.uk

Customers from outside the UK please telephone +44 1865 312262

Raintree is an imprint of Capstone Global Library Limited,
a company incorporated in England and Wales having its registered office at 7 Pilgrim
Street, London, EC4V 6LB
– Registered company number: 6695582

First published by © Stone Arch Books in 2011
First published in the United Kingdom
in paperback in 2012
The moral rights of the proprietor have been asserted.

Art Director: Bob Lentz
Designer: Hilary Wacholz
Production Specialist: Michelle Biedschied
Editor: Catherine Veitch
Originated by Capstone Global Library Ltd
Printed and bound in China by Leo Paper Products Ltd

ISBN 978 1 406 22658 4
15 14 13 12 11
10 9 8 7 6 5 4 3 2 1

British Library Cataloguing in Publication Data
A full catalogue record for this book is available
from the British Library.

She lived with a cat, a dog, and a mouse.

The cat, the dog, and the mouse were a lazy bunch.

They slept all day while the little red
hen worked.

She did all of the cooking, cleaning, and gardening.

One day, while she was in the garden, the little red hen found some grains of wheat.

PEAS

CARROTS

BEANS

"Who will help me plant this wheat?"
she asked.

"Not I!" said the cat.

"Not I!" said the dog.

"Not I!" said the mouse.

"Then I guess I will do it myself," said the little red hen.

So she planted the wheat and helped it grow.

When the wheat was ready, the little red hen asked, "Who will help me cut this wheat?"

"Not I!" was the reply.

"Then I guess I will do it myself!"
she said.

So the little red hen cut the wheat herself.

After the wheat was cut, the little red hen said, "This wheat must be ground into flour. Who will take it to the mill?"

Again she heard, "Not I!"

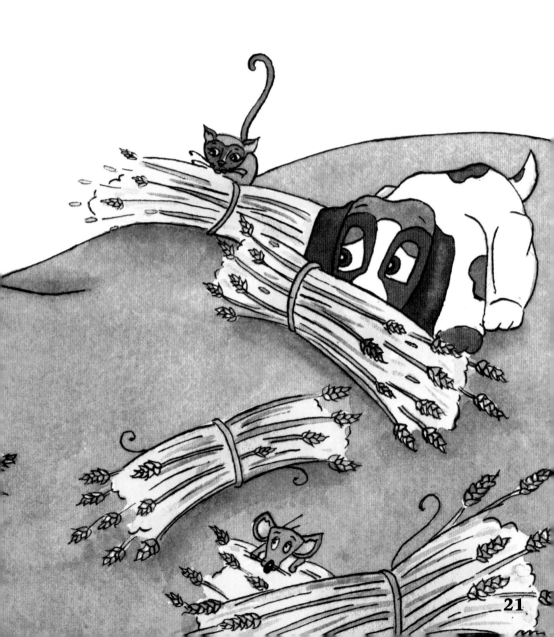

"Then I guess I will do it myself," she said, with a sigh.

So the little red hen took the wheat to the mill. She returned with a big sack of flour.

23

"Who will help me make bread from this flour?" she asked.

"Not I!" shouted the cat.

"Not I!" shouted the dog.

"Not I!" shouted the mouse.

The little red hen muttered, "Then I guess
I will do it myself."

She spent the whole afternoon baking bread.

When the bread was done, the little red hen asked, "Who will help me eat this bread?"

"I will!" yelled the cat.

"I will!" yelled the dog.

"I will!" yelled the mouse.

"I don't think so. I have done everything else myself. I will eat this bread myself, too," the little red hen said with a smile.

And she ate every last crumb all by herself.

The End